For Annie and Jimmy

THE MANY ADVENTURES OF
Johnny Mutton

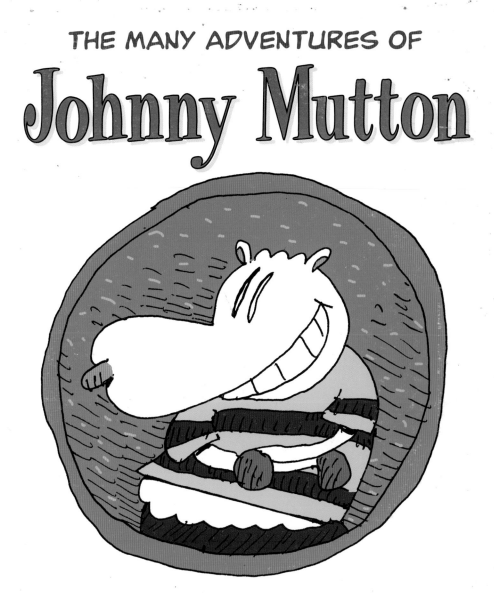

STORIES AND PICTURES
BY JAMES PROIMOS

MAR . 7 2002

HARCOURT, INC.

SAN DIEGO   NEW YORK   LONDON

Requests for permission to make copies of any part of the work should
be mailed to the following address: Permissions Department, Harcourt, Inc.,
6277 Sea Harbor Drive, Orlando, Florida 32887-6777.

www.harcourt.com

Library of Congress Cataloging-in-Publication Data
Proimos, James.
The many adventures of Johnny Mutton/stories and pictures by James Proimos.
p.   cm.
Summary: Although he is a sheep, Johnny Mutton goes to school, competes
in the spelling bee, dresses up for Halloween, and discovers his favorite
sport, always remaining true to himself.
[1. Sheep—Fiction.   2. Schools—Fiction.   3. Individuality—Fiction.]
I. Title.
PZ7.P9432Man   2001
[Fic]—dc21   00-9219
ISBN 0-15-202379-8   ISBN 0-15-204413-1 (pb)

First edition

A C E G H F D B
A C E G H F D B (pb)

Printed in Hong Kong

The illustrations in this book were first drawn with a pen,
then colorized in Adobe Photoshop.
The display type was set in Heatwave.
The text type was set in Sand.
Printed by South China Printing Company, Ltd., Hong Kong
This book was printed on totally chlorine-free Nymolla Matte Art paper.
Production supervision by Sandra Grebenar and Ginger Boyer
Designed by Kaelin Chappell and James Proimos
Jacket/cover designed by Barry Age

The Stories

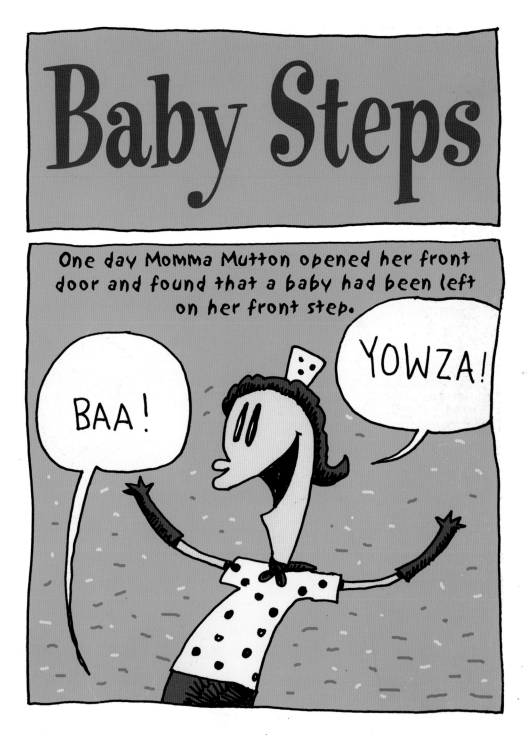

But it wasn't just any baby.

It was a baby...

...sheep!

Although Johnny often got those last two confused.

Momma did such a good job bringing up Johnny that although folks noticed he was different, no one noticed he was a sheep.

THERE'S SOMETHING ODD ABOUT THAT BOY.

MR. STOCKMAN

HE'S VERY HAPPY. MAYBE THAT'S WHAT MAKES HIM STAND OUT.

LORETTA SMATZ

HE DOESN'T EVEN TRY TO FIT IN. I DON'T LIKE THAT.

HE'S SO HIM.

MRS. TORPOLLI

I NOTICED HE WAS DIFFERENT RIGHT AWAY. HE'S A GOOD PETTER.

THE SMITHS' DOG

More Fun than a Bag of Marshmallows

Johnny Mutton couldn't wait for the first day he would ever go to school. When he walked into the classroom, all the kids immediately noticed he was different.

The students each brought their teacher, Mr. Slopdish, an apple.

THANK YOU ALL.

Johnny brought him a bag of marshmallows.

11

All the kids laughed.

And then Mr. Slopdish said...
BEING DIFFERENT IS VERY NICE, ESPECIALLY WHERE MARSHMALLOWS ARE INVOLVED.
GULP

But Johnny didn't hear that because he was in the closet, hiding from those creepy fake teeth.

17

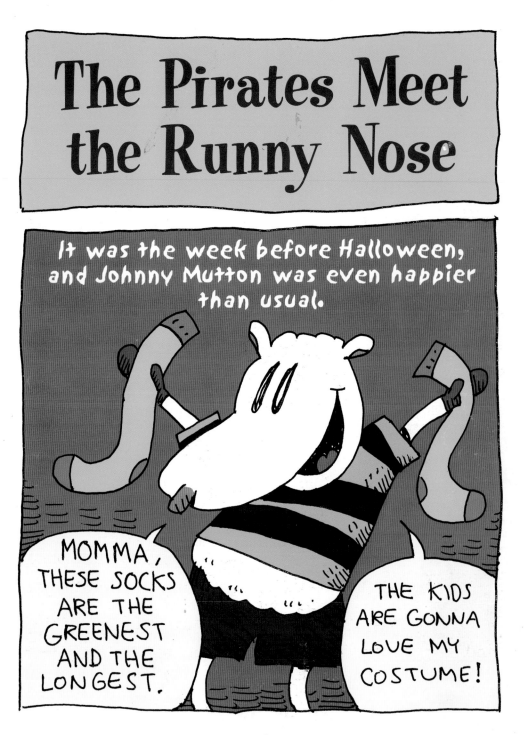

26

On Halloween morning, when Johnny ran down the stairs, he nearly scared Momma out of her wits.

Momma Mutton was a great basketball player.

She wanted Johnny Mutton to be a great basketball player, too. So every day she would throw him a hundred passes.

And every day a hundred passes would bounce off his fluffy body.

Actually, he did catch one of her passes. But it was an accident.

And that's exactly what he did.

Johnny Mutton went on to become a national hero by winning twenty gold medals in the Olympics for water ballet.

Mr. Slopdish wound up famous for telling stories about Johnny Mutton on TV talk shows. Eventually he became the Poofy Marshmallow spokesperson—his face on every bag.

They Now?

The Halloween after Johnny won those twenty gold medals, all the kids in this book dressed up as Johnny Mutton.

Except for Gloria Crust and Johnny Mutton, that is. Gloria dressed up as a mop. Johnny, as a nasty spill.

A FUZZY BUG

A WINDSHIELD WIPER

Momma continued to find many interesting items on her front step. But never again would she come across anything quite as wonderful as Johnny Mutton.

A FOUR-LEAF CLOVER

A DIAMOND RING

MONEY- BACK
GUARANTEE

A MONEY-BACK GUARANTEE

A DOLL'S SHOE